KELLOGG-HUBBARD
CHILDREN'S LIBRARY
135 Main Street
Montpelier, Vermont 05602
223-3338

THE WATER SHELL

Written and illustrated by

GRETCHEN SCHIELDS

GULLIVER BOOKS
HARCOURT BRACE & COMPANY
San Diego   New York   London

Copyright © 1995 by Gretchen Schields

All rights reserved. No part of this publication may be reproduced or
transmitted in any form or by any means, electronic or mechanical,
including photocopy, recording, or any information storage and retrieval
system, without permission in writing from the publisher.

Requests for permission to make copies of any part of the work
should be mailed to: Permissions Department, Harcourt Brace & Company,
6277 Sea Harbor Drive, Orlando, Florida 32887-6777.

Gulliver Books is a registered trademark of Harcourt Brace & Company.

Library of Congress Cataloging-in-Publication Data
Schields, Gretchen.
The Water Shell/Gretchen Schields.—1st ed.
p.   cm.
"Gulliver books."
Summary: Keiki seeks to retrieve the precious Water Shell,
which protects her Polynesian island home and
has been stolen by the Fire Queen.
ISBN 0-15-200404-1
[1. Polynesia—Fiction. 2. Fantasy.]
I. Title.
PZ7.S3455Wat   1995
[E]—dc20   94-15606

First edition
A B C D E

Printed in Singapore

The illustrations in this book were done in watercolor
on double-weight illustration board.
The display type was hand rendered by Judythe Sieck.
The text type was set in Cochin.
Color separations were made by Bright Arts, Ltd., Singapore.
Printed and bound by Tien Wah Press, Singapore
This book was printed with soya-based inks on Leykam recycled paper,
which contains more than 20 percent postconsumer waste and
has a total recycled content of at least 50 percent.
Production supervision by Warren Wallerstein and David Hough
Designed by Kaelin Chappell

*Thanks to my friend Amy Tan for writing
the wonderful stories that were our
first shared adventures in children's books,
and for encouraging me not only to draw
but to write my own stories*

Fond thanks to John Stevenson

*And special thanks to my editor,
Liz Van Doren, for helping me polish
those stories into books*

For the myths and magic
of the South Pacific

LONG AGO, WHEN THE WORLD STOOD STILL IN TIME, a little girl lived on Kua-i-Helani, a beautiful island that floated in a tropical sea. Nobody on the island could remember being older or younger than they were—or ever having been anywhere else. In this changeless paradise the little girl passed each day with her companions in the same pleasant way. They swam in the lagoon, played games among the bright flowers, and surfed on the white breaking waves. They ate sweet fruits and sang songs late into the lazy, warm nights.

Kua-i-Helani was a land made by magic. This magic was contained inside an egg that glowed in the ocean, deep, deep down. The egg was transparent, but all the shifting colors of the sea flowed inside it. The people knew the egg was there to keep them safe. They called it the Water Shell and they loved it because it protected them.

Beyond the perfect little world of Kua-i-Helani were great stretches of darkness and danger. The Fire Queen ruled over the darkness in fury and despair, cursing the island and its happiness. The Water Shell had once been hers. It had protected the Fire Queen and given her great power. But it had been taken from her, leaving her fierce and warlike, with a thirst for revenge.

One horrible day, while the people on Kua-i-Helani were dancing and singing their songs as usual, the soldiers of the Fire Queen erupted without warning from their seething universe. Screaming and clawing, they surged around the floating island. Earthquakes shook the huts down. Typhoons blew the flowers out to sea and flattened the trees. The people moaned and shrieked in fear as they watched the demon soldiers plunge down beneath the waves in search of the magical Water Shell. The raiders emerged in a fierce waterspout and whirled triumphantly away with the Water Shell in their claws. The one thing the people feared had come to pass.

From far away came a wailing sound. It grew louder and louder and became a roar. The sea swelled in a giant wall and a huge wave crashed upon the beaches. The little girl was caught in its crest and swept away.

When at last the churning wave stopped tumbling her about, the little girl found herself in a watery forest. Sea grasses waved in the currents. Big and little fishes swam among them.

The girl looked around her and saw, floating darkly above her, the great Shark of the Sea. In a deep, cold voice he spoke to her. "Child! The Water Shell alone kept your perfect world safe. It has been stolen by the Fire Queen! Now that she has the magic of the Water Shell, she has the power to escape from her dark kingdom and destroy your floating world.

"On the day your world was made," continued the Shark, "I swam through your dreams. I saw that you would be strong and brave. You must go to the Fire Queen and take back the Water Shell." He gazed at the child with his leaden eyes. "If you don't, your world will be gone forever. Make a choice."

"I want to go home!" cried the child.

"Then tear a tooth from my mouth," commanded the fearsome creature as he bared his gleaming jaws. The little girl recoiled in shock. She remembered the terrifying raid by the soldiers of the Fire Queen and how they carried away the Water Shell. She thought of the colored birds, the flowers, and the warm, soft sun of her home. *Could she keep it safe? She must at least try!*

Darting forward like a minnow, she reached between the rows of razor teeth and grasped at one. It did not resist her tug; nor did it cut her hand. She pulled it to her, one great curved tooth shaped and worked like a fishhook.

"I will go," she told the Shark, holding tightly on to his tooth.

"You have chosen wisely," rumbled the Shark. "When you must again make a choice, this charm will help you act." He swam closer. "Now I will give you your name. You are Keiki, which means 'child.'"

With a powerful lunge, the Shark disappeared. Keiki clutched the fish-hook tooth in her hand and began to swim.

Keiki swam and swam, upward through sun-shot depths into a dark rocky tunnel, a lava tube. After many turns and twists she came at last into the light of day. She was in a little pond ringed with ferns. She recognized it immediately. It was where she used to splash and play.

But Kua-i-Helani was so changed! A huge smoking lava cone rose through the center of the island. Rivers of black lava had coursed down its slopes, sealing the green forests beneath a rocky plain. The people were gone; the flowers, too, and the birds. Ash fell mournfully around her.

"I must remember the way it was," said Keiki aloud to the little oasis in which she sat. "Otherwise I cannot go on."

"You must also have hope," piped a tiny voice, startling Keiki mightily. She peered into the ferns and saw a spiderweb and, dancing on its strands, a little yellow spider.

"Remembering is about looking back. Hope is about looking forward. Hope is fragile, like my web," chirped the spider. "But anchored to the right points, and woven well, it is very strong!" She twanged the shining strands of her web as proof. "Here, I will give you a present that will help you remember that. Use it wisely." The spider busily spun out a length of silken web and blew it toward Keiki.

Keiki caught the silken thread and, slipping it through the hole in the Shark's tooth, she hung it like a necklace round her neck.

"I've been waiting for you! I know who you are—Keiki, the child!" the spider went on. She waggled a red-tipped leg at Keiki. "The Fire Queen has the Water Shell up in her mountain. That's where you must go! Only you can stop her!"

"Oh, Spider!" Keiki cried as she gazed up at the smoking volcano. "Even if I can get the Water Shell from the Fire Queen, what good can it do now? She has destroyed so much!"

"Trust what you love. It will take you where you need to go," chirped the little spider.

Keiki remembered Kua-i-Helani and all of its beautiful colors, which she had loved so much. Slowly, mistily, in shifting layers, a rainbow of just such colors rose from the pond waters around Keiki's feet. It arched up, up to the clouds that ringed the volcano.

"Go now," said the spider.

Keiki tested the rainbow with her toe. Its shimmering surface was solid! Without looking back she leaped onto the colored bridge.

Bing! Ting! Bong! Each colored band rang with a different musical note. Keiki hopped from red to violet, and violet to blue, blue to melodious green. With each sound Keiki's hope grew, and in this tuneful way, she danced up into the clouds.

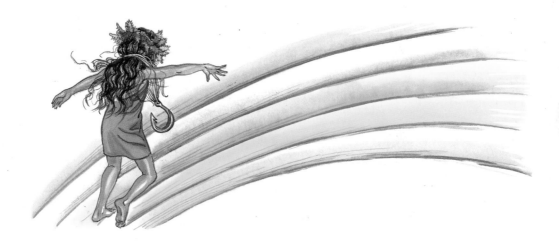

Vapors swirled around Keiki as she left the last tinkling bands of the rainbow bridge behind. She felt her way through the mists of a steamy, cloud-filled land. Ancient trees and creepers dripped in the dimness, and she heard the sound of streams and waterfalls flowing by her.

At the foot of a cascading waterfall, Keiki came upon three beautiful warrior women who were shaking droplets of water from their long hair. They wore fragrant necklaces made of flowers, seeds, and vines. With graceful movements of their hands and bodies, they danced the words of a song.

They called for Keiki to join them. "Sweet child! Brave child! Come to us!" They reached out with their dancing hands and drew her to them, through veils of falling water.

"We are great chieftesses, the Maidens of the Mist," they told her. "Our home is in the high, snowy places and the streams and waterfalls that flow from them. We know why you are here.

"We know the Fire Queen, too. Do you know that the Water Shell was once a part of her? She used its magic for selfish power and it was taken from her. She was cast out, and her anger grew and grew. Once our powers of ice and snow could hold her back, but now that she has stolen the Water Shell, she is too strong for us.

"You have seen what she has done. You must take back the Water Shell."

One maiden stepped forward. She held out a brilliant white cape from which came waves of cool air. "We will give you what help we can, brave child. Here is a gift to protect you from the flame of the Fire Queen's realm." She laid the snowy mantle at Keiki's feet. Then the dancing hands of the maidens waved farewell, and the warm tropic air became cold as they faded into the falling water and disappeared.

Keiki was left alone in the dripping forest. She picked up the cool white cape and walked forward into the mist.

"I did not!"

"You did too! You did! You did! You did!"

Keiki heard a loud argument ringing through the curling drafts of mist. She waded forward until she came upon two fabulously tattooed children yelling at each other. They had big fans in their hands and were whipping them back and forth, stirring up gusts of wind.

"Hello! Hello! Hello!" they shouted upon seeing Keiki. They dropped their fans and tumbled to her side. Interrupting each other's words, they told her that they were the Wind Children who fanned up the winds that whooshed around the world, who piled up the clouds, who stirred up storms, and who energetically kept everything in motion.

Then they demanded to know Keiki's story.

"Adventure!" they exclaimed with admiration when she had finished.

"Enemy soldiers!"

"A tidal wave!"

"The Shark of the Sea!"

"Fireworks! Eruptions! Explosions! Earthquakes!"

They asked Keiki why she would want everything to return to the way it had been, when nothing ever happened and nobody ever changed. Wasn't life much more exciting now, to go adventuring like she was, meeting danger head-on, living by her wits? Before Keiki could answer any of their questions, the Wind Children announced that, in fact, they would like to keep this interesting girl to live with them forever in their whirling Wind House!

Keiki protested that she must go, but the Wind Children would have none of it, insisting that the three of them could whip together the most thunderous storms and the most splendid clouds. They made her repeat the magic chant that would call up the storm winds, and they thrust a magic kite, shaped like a hawk, into her hands. This, they enthusiastically assured her, would carry her high into the sky—to where she could admire the excellent clouds they all would make.

As entertaining as the Wind Children were, Keiki knew she must escape from their cheerful clutches. She asked them to show her how they used their fans to whip up a wind. Delighted, the Wind Children began waving their giant fans with such energy that they produced a whirlwind. Keiki quickly stepped into it and was swirled away like a leaf.

Keiki's head was still spinning from the whirlwind ride when her feet touched down. The ground beneath her throbbed and rumbled as if it were a giant, breathing animal. Keiki knew that she had finally reached the realm of the Fire Queen.

She took a shaky step toward the rim of the volcano. Steam hissed up through cracks in the cinder crust. Keiki gasped. She was gazing down into the very heart of the earth, a crater that bubbled and boiled, a cauldron of fire.

Sulfurous fumes stung Keiki's eyes. Rings and rings of scaly birds, insects, dragons, and goblins spiraled around her. These were the soldiers of the Fire Queen, who had carried the Water Shell away! But Keiki had not come to see them.

"Come forward, cowardly Queen!" she shouted in a rage. "Why do you hide behind your soldiers? You are the real thief! It is you I've come to see!"

The soldiers vanished in a coil of smoke, their cackling calls lost in the roar of the volcano.

Lava exploded in a column and hung flaming in the air before falling in glowing chunks back into the pit. In its place burned the outline of a beautiful woman. The vision glimmered and gained substance, and as the shifting vapors parted, Keiki saw a blazing crown of red flowers. It was the Fire Queen.

She stretched out her hands toward Keiki and spoke.

"My child," she whispered, and her words, so surprisingly soft and caressing, sent a thrill through Keiki. "My dear little child!" The queen smiled, her teeth glowing like flames. "You are so clever and brave to have made this long journey! You are my guest, and you please me so! Let me welcome you!" She reached out to Keiki. As if in a dream, Keiki slowly raised her own hand in reply.

"You see me now as I truly am," sighed the queen, her eyes locked on Keiki's own. "For so long I was injured, wronged. I wandered weak and incomplete. But now I am whole again! The Water Shell is mine. My power is restored!"

The queen lifted her many flower necklaces, and Keiki saw the Water Shell. It glowed with a pure blue light in the breast of the Fire Queen, in place of her heart!

The sight shattered Keiki's trance. Pulling back her hand, she clutched the white mantle tightly about her and cried out, "You have stolen the power of the Water Shell! You have destroyed Kua-i-Helani!"

The Fire Queen threw back her head and laughed, wild peals of laughter that shook the mountainside. She touched the magic egg that was her heart and pointed at Keiki. "Child, Kua-i-Helani was a dreamworld that existed only through stolen magic—*magic stolen from me!* The Water Shell is mine now and I will do as I please with it! I have destroyed your useless world and in its place I have created a new one. Weak child of a vanished land! This is my world! You cannot claim it!"

Standing on the summit of the cinder cone that rose above the ruins of her home, Keiki realized that her perfect world was gone forever. But she had survived, and she had found the Water Shell. If there was to be a new world, it would be hers, too! She *would* claim it!

Keiki ripped the necklace of spider silk from her neck and, in one smooth toss, cast the fishhook at the Fire Queen's heart. Her aim was true! She tore the magic egg from the flaming breast of the Fire Queen and pulled it to her, then turned and ran.

The queen screamed in fury. Fountains of fire exploded from the empty place where the Water Shell had been. Sparks shot from her fingertips. Her snaking black hair coiled and twisted in smoking tangles.

Hugging the Water Shell close, Keiki ran through the firestorm. Roaring steam and sheets of fire enveloped her. Shielded by the white mantle, Keiki cried out the words to the Wind Children's chant. A cool breeze coursed through the heat and caught the wings of the Wind Children's kite. As the kite pulled Keiki into the air, she ripped the white mantle from her shoulders and flung it back into the flaming crater.

The volcano below shook with earthquakes as the icy mantle unleashed snowstorms that covered the cinder slopes with ice. Eruptions of lava froze in their course. The boiling crater hissed and hardened and then fell silent under a mantle of snow. The Fire Queen was sealed inside her own flaming realm.

The kite soared silently down the snow-covered slopes of the volcano and came to rest on the barren lava plain. Waves beat against the rocky shoreline. Small tongues of flame still flickered where streams of lava had recently flowed.

Charred, smoking tree stumps were all that remained of the forests and flowers of Kua-i-Helani. Was *this* the new world that she had vowed to claim? Keiki studied the Water Shell cradled in her arms. Its magic had once made this land a paradise. What magic did it have now?

Keiki sank to her knees. By her hand lay a sharp flint. Taking it up, Keiki cut away her long, thick hair and wove a nest from its strands. Into this she laid the glowing Water Shell, with its colors that shifted and swirled.

Suddenly the magic egg quivered. Small cracks crisscrossed its surface. It was hatching!

The Water Shell shuddered, then split in two. Water poured forth. It flowed upon the parched rock and into crevices, sprouting seeds that had been blown across the sea by the winds. The water rose into a misty rainbow in the sky, forming great clouds that rained down on the land in fertile showers. Forests and flowers sprang up from the rocky land. Trees ripened with fruit that became food for the birds that filled the skies. Fish flocked to the lagoons. Coral reefs grew in the sea.

The world that the Water Shell's magic had kept locked in an unchanging paradise had been destroyed. But Keiki had set the magic free. She watched in wonder as this new world surged around her, a panorama of energy and growth.

Keiki saw her face reflected in the water, now the face of a young woman. She was no longer a child in an unchanging world. That had been her past. This pulsing world of hope and choice—of birth and death and rebirth—had become her present. Keiki looked up from the nest where the shiny fragments of the Water Shell glowed, empty of their magic waters that now flowed freely through the world. She knew she would live and grow—with this new world that she had claimed—into her future.

A NOTE FROM THE AUTHOR

Polynesia means "many islands," and the region called Polynesia in the South Pacific Ocean includes the island groups of Tahiti, Hawaii, the Marquesas, the Society Islands, Samoa, Easter Island, and New Zealand.

Arriving from islands to the west, where they had migrated from Asia, people began to colonize the western part of Polynesia probably about 3,000 years ago. It was in the isolated island groups of Samoa and Tonga that the Polynesian language, culture, and ethnic appearance began to take on their unique forms.

As the population of the islands grew to be greater than their resources, some of the people continued to move on in large, oceangoing canoes. Navigating by the stars and ocean currents, they settled various islands. They carried their myths and legends with them in a scrupulously preserved oral history. As a result, there is a common thread that runs throughout the folklore of the South Pacific. It is from the imagery in these stories that many of the characters and themes of *The Water Shell* are derived.

Keiki's home, the mythical floating island of Kua-i-Helani, was said to drift about in the legendary region of Havaiki, the ancient far-western fatherland of the Polynesian people. In their migrations through the islands, the Polynesians carried with them the name of their ancestral home, Havaiki, and so called their new homes names like Hawaii, Kahiki, Tahiti, and Savaiiki that derived from Havaiki.

Keiki, the name given the little girl by the Shark, means "child" in the Hawaiian language. In Hawaiian myths a pregnant woman who is visited in her dreams by a shark will bear a magical child.

The fishhook has magical properties in Polynesian folklore. With a fishhook made from the jawbone of his grandmother, the demigod Maui fished up the chain of the Hawaiian islands from the ocean floor. This act of creation is mirrored in Keiki's snagging the Water Shell from its place in the Fire Queen's heart, freeing it to hatch a new world.

Maui was born prematurely to his mother, Hina. Thinking he was dead, Hina cut off her hair and wrapped him in it, just as Keiki makes a shroud for the egg with her own shorn locks.

The Fire Queen is based on Pele, Hawaii's best-known deity, the goddess of the volcano. (In some stories she is sister to the Shark.) Her dual aspects of destruction through fire and creation through the building of islands with her lava flows are reflected in *The Water Shell.*

The tattooed Wind Children, their Wind House, fans, and kites derive from the Maori, the Polynesian people who settled New Zealand. The Hawaiian trickster god Maui, who fished up the islands, also flew his kite, commanding the winds with a chant to make it soar. Tattooing is said to have been brought up from the underworld to the Maori people by a man called Mataora, and the art form is known as *moko* for the lizard whose curling tail its fantastic designs imitate.

In Hawaiian folklore the Maidens of the Mist were beautiful queens, wise and adventurous. They were enemies of Pele and ruled the high mountains north of Hawaii's Kilauea volcano. The maidens represent the eternal warfare between fire and ice, as evidenced by the burning lava and the veils of snow that they sometimes send to cover the slopes of the neighboring Mauna Kea, now dormant. Once, in a tremendous battle with Pele, Poliahu, the best known of the maidens, sealed that fiery queen's volcano and froze her lava rivers by throwing a snowy mantle of pure white *kapa*-cloth over the erupting mountain.

The maidens speak to Keiki through a traditional combination of dance and song called the hula. The rhythm and poetry of the hula help make it easier to memorize the elaborate Polynesian oral histories and genealogies.

The maidens and the Fire Queen wear leis, ritual adornments made from flowers, feathers, seeds, shells, leaves, and vines. Keiki wears a lei of young fern fronds (palapalai) in her hair, and the Fire Queen is crowned with a lei of red lehua blossoms, flowers sacred to the goddess Pele.

The Water Shell, whose magic powers are contained within its own shell, reflects origin myths from diverse cultures around the world. These myths share a theme of the egg as the primal universe from which all things will evolve once an action or choice has set in motion the process that initiates the creation of the world.